Thank You For

_____
_____
_____
_____

Date

People To Pray For

_____
_____
_____
_____
_____
_____
_____
_____
_____
_____
_____

Personal Challenges

_____
_____
_____
_____

Society And Government

_____
_____
_____
_____

Reflections

_____
_____
_____
_____

Thank You For

_____

_____

_____

_____

Personal Challenges

_____

_____

_____

_____

Society And Government

_____

_____

_____

_____

Reflections

_____

_____

_____

_____

_____

Date

_____

People To Pray For

_____

_____

_____

_____

_____

_____

_____

_____

_____

_____

_____

Thank You For

_____

_____

_____

_____

Personal Challenges

_____

_____

_____

_____

Society And Government

_____

_____

_____

_____

Reflections

_____

_____

_____

_____

_____

Date

_____

People To Pray For

_____

_____

_____

_____

_____

_____

_____

_____

_____

Thank You For

_____
_____
_____
_____

Personal Challenges

_____
_____
_____
_____

Society And Government

_____
_____
_____
_____

Date

_____

People To Pray For

_____
_____
_____
_____
_____
_____
_____
_____
_____
_____

Reflections

_____
_____
_____
_____
_____

Thank You For

_____
_____
_____
_____

Date

_____

People To Pray For

_____
_____
_____
_____
_____
_____
_____
_____
_____
_____
_____

Personal Challenges

_____
_____
_____
_____

Society And Government

_____
_____
_____
_____

Reflections

_____
_____
_____
_____
_____

Thank You For

_____
_____
_____
_____

Personal Challenges

_____
_____
_____
_____
_____

Society And Government

_____
_____
_____
_____

Date

_____

People To Pray For

_____
_____
_____
_____
_____
_____
_____
_____
_____
_____
_____
_____

Reflections

_____
_____
_____
_____
_____

Thank You For

_____

_____

_____

_____

Personal Challenges

_____

_____

_____

_____

Society And Government

_____

_____

_____

_____

Reflections

_____

_____

_____

_____

Date

_____

People To Pray For

_____

_____

_____

_____

_____

_____

_____

_____

_____

_____

_____

_____

_____

Thank You For

_____
_____
_____
_____

Personal Challenges

_____
_____
_____
_____

Society And Government

_____
_____
_____
_____

Reflections

_____
_____
_____
_____

Date

_____

People To Pray For

_____
_____
_____
_____
_____
_____
_____
_____
_____
_____
_____

Thank You For

_____
_____
_____
_____

Personal Challenges

_____
_____
_____
_____

Society And Government

_____
_____
_____
_____

Date

_____

People To Pray For

_____
_____
_____
_____
_____
_____
_____
_____
_____
_____
_____

Reflections

_____
_____
_____
_____
_____

Thank You For

_____
_____
_____
_____

Personal Challenges

_____
_____
_____
_____

Society And Government

_____
_____
_____
_____

Reflections

_____
_____
_____
_____
_____

Date

_____

People To Pray For

_____
_____
_____
_____
_____
_____
_____
_____
_____
_____

Thank You For

_____
_____
_____
_____

Date

_____

People To Pray For

_____
_____
_____
_____
_____
_____
_____
_____
_____
_____
_____
_____
_____

Personal Challenges

_____
_____
_____
_____

Society And Government

_____
_____
_____
_____

Reflections

_____
_____
_____
_____
_____

Thank You For

_____
_____
_____
_____

Personal Challenges

_____
_____
_____
_____

Society And Government

_____
_____
_____
_____

Reflections

_____
_____
_____
_____

Date

_____

People To Pray For

_____
_____
_____
_____
_____
_____
_____
_____
_____
_____

Thank You For

_____
_____
_____
_____

Date

_____

People To Pray For

_____
_____
_____
_____
_____
_____
_____
_____
_____
_____
_____
_____

Personal Challenges

_____
_____
_____
_____

Society And Government

_____
_____
_____
_____

Reflections

_____
_____
_____
_____
_____

Thank You For

Date

People To Pray For

Personal Challenges

Society And Government

Reflections

Thank You For

_____
_____
_____
_____

Personal Challenges

_____
_____
_____
_____

Society And Government

_____
_____
_____
_____

Date

_____

People To Pray For

_____
_____
_____
_____
_____
_____
_____
_____
_____

Reflections

_____
_____
_____
_____
_____

Thank You For

_____
_____
_____
_____

Personal Challenges

_____
_____
_____
_____

Society And Government

_____
_____
_____
_____

Reflections

_____
_____
_____
_____
_____

Date

_____

People To Pray For

_____
_____
_____
_____
_____
_____
_____
_____
_____
_____
_____

Thank You For

_____
_____
_____
_____
_____

Personal Challenges

_____
_____
_____
_____

Society And Government

_____
_____
_____
_____

Date

_____

People To Pray For

_____
_____
_____
_____
_____
_____
_____
_____
_____
_____

Reflections

_____
_____
_____
_____
_____

Thank You For

Date

People To Pray For

Personal Challenges

Society And Government

Reflections

Thank You For

_____
_____
_____
_____

Date

_____

People To Pray For

_____
_____
_____
_____
_____
_____
_____
_____
_____
_____
_____
_____

Personal Challenges

_____
_____
_____
_____

Society And Government

_____
_____
_____
_____

Reflections

_____
_____
_____
_____
_____

Thank You For

Date

People To Pray For

Personal Challenges

Society And Government

Reflections

Thank You For

_____

_____

_____

_____

Personal Challenges

_____

_____

_____

_____

Society And Government

_____

_____

_____

_____

Reflections

_____

_____

_____

_____

Date

_____

People To Pray For

_____

_____

_____

_____

_____

_____

_____

_____

_____

_____

_____

_____

_____

Thank You For

Date

Personal Challenges

People To Pray For

Society And Government

Reflections

Thank You For

_____
_____
_____
_____

Personal Challenges

_____
_____
_____
_____

Society And Government

_____
_____
_____
_____

Reflections

_____
_____
_____
_____

Date

_____

People To Pray For

_____
_____
_____
_____
_____
_____
_____
_____
_____
_____

Thank You For

_____

_____

_____

_____

Personal Challenges

_____

_____

_____

_____

Society And Government

_____

_____

_____

_____

Reflections

_____

_____

_____

_____

_____

Date

_____

People To Pray For

_____

_____

_____

_____

_____

_____

_____

_____

_____

_____

Thank You For

_____
_____
_____
_____

Personal Challenges

_____
_____
_____
_____

Society And Government

_____
_____
_____
_____

Date

_____

People To Pray For

_____
_____
_____
_____
_____
_____
_____
_____
_____
_____

Reflections

_____
_____
_____
_____
_____

Thank You For

_____

_____

_____

_____

Personal Challenges

_____

_____

_____

_____

Society And Government

_____

_____

_____

_____

Reflections

_____

_____

_____

_____

Date

_____

People To Pray For

_____

_____

_____

_____

_____

_____

_____

_____

_____

Thank You For

_____

_____

_____

_____

Date

_____

People To Pray For

_____

_____

_____

_____

_____

_____

_____

_____

Personal Challenges

_____

_____

_____

_____

Society And Government

_____

_____

_____

_____

Reflections

_____

_____

_____

_____

_____

Thank You For

Date

Personal Challenges

People To Pray For

Society And Government

Reflections

Thank You For

_____

_____

_____

Personal Challenges

_____

_____

_____

_____

Society And Government

_____

_____

_____

Date

_____

People To Pray For

_____

_____

_____

_____

_____

_____

_____

_____

_____

_____

Reflections

_____

_____

_____

_____

Thank You For

_____
_____
_____
_____

Personal Challenges

_____
_____
_____
_____
_____

Society And Government

_____
_____
_____
_____

Date

_____

People To Pray For

_____
_____
_____
_____
_____
_____
_____
_____
_____
_____
_____

Reflections

_____
_____
_____
_____
_____

Thank You For

_____
_____
_____
_____

Personal Challenges

_____
_____
_____
_____

Society And Government

_____
_____
_____
_____

Date

_____

People To Pray For

_____
_____
_____
_____
_____
_____
_____
_____
_____
_____

Reflections

_____
_____
_____
_____
_____

Thank You For

Date

Personal Challenges

People To Pray For

Society And Government

Reflections

Thank You For

_____
_____
_____
_____

Date

_____

People To Pray For

_____
_____
_____
_____
_____
_____
_____
_____
_____
_____
_____
_____

Personal Challenges

_____
_____
_____
_____

Society And Government

_____
_____
_____
_____

Reflections

_____
_____
_____
_____
_____

Thank You For

_____

_____

_____

_____

Personal Challenges

_____

_____

_____

_____

Society And Government

_____

_____

_____

_____

Reflections

_____

_____

_____

_____

Date

_____

People To Pray For

_____

_____

_____

_____

_____

_____

_____

_____

_____

_____

_____

_____

Thank You For

_____
_____
_____
_____

Date

_____

People To Pray For

_____
_____
_____
_____
_____
_____
_____
_____
_____
_____

Personal Challenges

_____
_____
_____
_____

Society And Government

_____
_____
_____
_____

Reflections

_____
_____
_____
_____
_____

Thank You For

_____
_____
_____
_____

Personal Challenges

_____
_____
_____
_____

Society And Government

_____
_____
_____
_____

Reflections

_____
_____
_____
_____

Date

_____

People To Pray For

_____
_____
_____
_____
_____
_____
_____
_____
_____

Thank You For

_____
_____
_____
_____

Date

_____

People To Pray For

_____
_____
_____
_____
_____
_____
_____
_____
_____
_____
_____

Personal Challenges

_____
_____
_____
_____

Society And Government

_____
_____
_____
_____

Reflections

_____
_____
_____
_____

Thank You For

_____

_____

_____

_____

Personal Challenges

_____

_____

_____

_____

Society And Government

_____

_____

_____

_____

Reflections

_____

_____

_____

_____

_____

Date

_____

People To Pray For

_____

_____

_____

_____

_____

_____

_____

_____

_____

_____

_____

_____

Thank You For

_____
_____
_____
_____

Personal Challenges

_____
_____
_____
_____

Society And Government

_____
_____
_____
_____

Date

_____

People To Pray For

_____
_____
_____
_____
_____
_____
_____
_____
_____
_____
_____

Reflections

_____
_____
_____
_____

Thank You For

_____
_____
_____
_____

Personal Challenges

_____
_____
_____
_____

Society And Government

_____
_____
_____
_____

Reflections

_____
_____
_____
_____

Date

_____

People To Pray For

_____
_____
_____
_____
_____
_____
_____
_____
_____

Thank You For

_____
_____
_____
_____

Personal Challenges

_____
_____
_____
_____

Society And Government

_____
_____
_____
_____

Date

_____

People To Pray For

_____
_____
_____
_____
_____
_____
_____
_____
_____
_____

Reflections

_____
_____
_____
_____
_____

Thank You For

_____

_____

_____

_____

Personal Challenges

_____

_____

_____

_____

Society And Government

_____

_____

_____

_____

Reflections

_____

_____

_____

_____

Date

_____

People To Pray For

_____

_____

_____

_____

_____

_____

_____

_____

_____

Thank You For

_____

_____

_____

_____

Personal Challenges

_____

_____

_____

_____

Society And Government

_____

_____

_____

_____

Reflections

_____

_____

_____

_____

Date

_____

People To Pray For

_____

_____

_____

_____

_____

_____

_____

_____

_____

_____

_____

Thank You For

Date

Personal Challenges

People To Pray For

Society And Government

Reflections

Thank You For

_____
_____
_____
_____

Personal Challenges

_____
_____
_____
_____

Society And Government

_____
_____
_____

Date

_____

People To Pray For

_____
_____
_____
_____
_____
_____
_____
_____
_____
_____

Reflections

_____
_____
_____
_____

Thank You For

_____
_____
_____
_____

Personal Challenges

_____
_____
_____
_____

Society And Government

_____
_____
_____
_____

Reflections

_____
_____
_____
_____

Date

_____

People To Pray For

_____
_____
_____
_____
_____
_____
_____
_____
_____
_____

Thank You For

_____
_____
_____
_____

Personal Challenges

_____
_____
_____
_____

Society And Government

_____
_____
_____
_____

Date

_____

People To Pray For

_____
_____
_____
_____
_____
_____
_____
_____
_____
_____

Reflections

_____
_____
_____
_____
_____

Thank You For

Date

People To Pray For

Personal Challenges

Society And Government

Reflections

Thank You For

_____

_____

_____

_____

Personal Challenges

_____

_____

_____

_____

Society And Government

_____

_____

_____

_____

Date

_____

People To Pray For

_____

_____

_____

_____

_____

_____

_____

_____

_____

_____

_____

Reflections

_____

_____

_____

_____

_____

Thank You For

_____
_____
_____
_____

Personal Challenges

_____
_____
_____
_____

Society And Government

_____
_____
_____
_____

Date

_____

People To Pray For

_____
_____
_____
_____
_____
_____
_____
_____
_____
_____
_____

Reflections

_____
_____
_____
_____

Thank You For

_____

_____

_____

_____

Personal Challenges

_____

_____

_____

_____

Society And Government

_____

_____

_____

_____

Date

_____

People To Pray For

_____

_____

_____

_____

_____

_____

_____

_____

_____

_____

_____

_____

Reflections

_____

_____

_____

_____

_____

Thank You For

_____
_____
_____
_____

Personal Challenges

_____
_____
_____
_____
_____

Society And Government

_____
_____
_____
_____

Reflections

_____
_____
_____
_____
_____

Date

_____

People To Pray For

_____
_____
_____
_____
_____
_____
_____
_____
_____
_____
_____

Thank You For

_____
_____
_____
_____

Personal Challenges

_____
_____
_____
_____

Society And Government

_____
_____
_____
_____

Date

_____

People To Pray For

_____
_____
_____
_____
_____
_____
_____
_____
_____
_____

Reflections

_____
_____
_____
_____

Thank You For

_____
_____
_____
_____

Personal Challenges

_____
_____
_____
_____

Society And Government

_____
_____
_____
_____

Reflections

_____
_____
_____
_____

Date

_____

People To Pray For

_____
_____
_____
_____
_____
_____
_____
_____
_____
_____

Thank You For

_____

_____

_____

_____

Personal Challenges

_____

_____

_____

_____

Society And Government

_____

_____

_____

_____

Date

_____

People To Pray For

_____

_____

_____

_____

_____

_____

_____

_____

_____

_____

Reflections

_____

_____

_____

_____

Thank You For

_____

_____

_____

_____

Personal Challenges

_____

_____

_____

_____

Society And Government

_____

_____

_____

_____

Reflections

_____

_____

_____

_____

_____

Date

_____

People To Pray For

_____

_____

_____

_____

_____

_____

_____

_____

_____

_____

_____

Thank You For

Date

Personal Challenges

People To Pray For

Society And Government

Reflections

Thank You For

_____

_____

_____

_____

Personal Challenges

_____

_____

_____

_____

Society And Government

_____

_____

_____

_____

Reflections

_____

_____

_____

_____

Date

_____

People To Pray For

_____

_____

_____

_____

_____

_____

_____

_____

_____

_____

_____

_____

Thank You For

_____

_____

_____

_____

Personal Challenges

_____

_____

_____

_____

Society And Government

_____

_____

_____

_____

Date

_____

People To Pray For

_____

_____

_____

_____

_____

_____

_____

_____

_____

_____

Reflections

_____

_____

_____

_____

_____

Thank You For

_____
_____
_____
_____

Personal Challenges

_____
_____
_____
_____
_____

Society And Government

_____
_____
_____
_____

Reflections

_____
_____
_____
_____
_____

Date

_____

People To Pray For

_____
_____
_____
_____
_____
_____
_____
_____
_____
_____

Thank You For

_____
_____
_____
_____

Personal Challenges

_____
_____
_____
_____

Society And Government

_____
_____
_____
_____

Date

_____

People To Pray For

_____
_____
_____
_____
_____
_____
_____
_____
_____
_____
_____

Reflections

_____
_____
_____
_____
_____

Thank You For

_____

_____

_____

_____

Personal Challenges

_____

_____

_____

_____

_____

Society And Government

_____

_____

_____

_____

Date

_____

People To Pray For

_____

_____

_____

_____

_____

_____

_____

_____

_____

_____

_____

Reflections

_____

_____

_____

_____

_____

Thank You For

Date

People To Pray For

Personal Challenges

Society And Government

Reflections

Thank You For

_____

_____

_____

Personal Challenges

_____

_____

_____

Society And Government

_____

_____

_____

Reflections

_____

_____

_____

_____

Date

_____

People To Pray For

_____

_____

_____

_____

_____

_____

_____

_____

_____

Thank You For

Date

Personal Challenges

People To Pray For

Society And Government

Reflections

Thank You For

_____
_____
_____
_____

Personal Challenges

_____
_____
_____
_____

Society And Government

_____
_____
_____
_____

Date

_____

People To Pray For

_____
_____
_____
_____
_____
_____
_____
_____
_____
_____

Reflections

_____
_____
_____
_____

Thank You For

Date

People To Pray For

Personal Challenges

Society And Government

Reflections

Thank You For

_____

_____

_____

_____

Personal Challenges

_____

_____

_____

_____

Society And Government

_____

_____

_____

_____

Reflections

_____

_____

_____

_____

Date

_____

People To Pray For

_____

_____

_____

_____

_____

_____

_____

_____

_____

_____

Thank You For

_____
_____
_____
_____

Personal Challenges

_____
_____
_____
_____
_____

Society And Government

_____
_____
_____
_____

Date

_____

People To Pray For

_____
_____
_____
_____
_____
_____
_____
_____
_____
_____
_____
_____

Reflections

_____
_____
_____
_____
_____

Thank You For

_____

_____

_____

_____

Personal Challenges

_____

_____

_____

_____

Society And Government

_____

_____

_____

_____

Date

_____

People To Pray For

_____

_____

_____

_____

_____

_____

_____

_____

_____

_____

_____

Reflections

_____

_____

_____

_____

_____

Thank You For

Date

Personal Challenges

People To Pray For

Society And Government

Reflections

Thank You For

_____

_____

_____

_____

Personal Challenges

_____

_____

_____

_____

Society And Government

_____

_____

_____

_____

Reflections

_____

_____

_____

_____

Date

_____

People To Pray For

_____

_____

_____

_____

_____

_____

_____

_____

_____

_____

Thank You For

_____
_____
_____
_____

Personal Challenges

_____
_____
_____
_____

Society And Government

_____
_____
_____
_____

Reflections

_____
_____
_____
_____

Date

_____

People To Pray For

_____
_____
_____
_____
_____
_____
_____
_____
_____
_____

Thank You For

_____
_____
_____
_____

Personal Challenges

_____
_____
_____
_____

Society And Government

_____
_____
_____
_____

Reflections

_____
_____
_____
_____

Date

_____

People To Pray For

_____
_____
_____
_____
_____
_____
_____
_____
_____
_____
_____

Thank You For

_____

_____

_____

_____

Personal Challenges

_____

_____

_____

_____

Society And Government

_____

_____

_____

_____

Reflections

_____

_____

_____

_____

Date

_____

People To Pray For

_____

_____

_____

_____

_____

_____

_____

_____

_____

_____

Thank You For

_____
_____
_____
_____

Personal Challenges

_____
_____
_____
_____

Society And Government

_____
_____
_____
_____

Reflections

_____
_____
_____
_____

Date

_____

People To Pray For

_____
_____
_____
_____
_____
_____
_____
_____
_____

Thank You For

_____
_____
_____
_____

Personal Challenges

_____
_____
_____
_____

Society And Government

_____
_____
_____
_____

Date

_____

People To Pray For

_____
_____
_____
_____
_____
_____
_____
_____
_____
_____

Reflections

_____
_____
_____
_____
_____

Thank You For

_____
_____
_____
_____

Personal Challenges

_____
_____
_____
_____
_____

Society And Government

_____
_____
_____
_____

Reflections

_____
_____
_____
_____
_____

Date

_____

People To Pray For

_____
_____
_____
_____
_____
_____
_____
_____
_____
_____

Thank You For

_____
_____
_____
_____

Personal Challenges

_____
_____
_____
_____

Society And Government

_____
_____
_____
_____

Date

_____
_____

People To Pray For

_____
_____
_____
_____
_____
_____
_____
_____
_____
_____

Reflections

_____
_____
_____
_____
_____

Thank You For

_____
_____
_____
_____

Personal Challenges

_____
_____
_____
_____

Society And Government

_____
_____
_____
_____

Date

_____

People To Pray For

_____
_____
_____
_____
_____
_____
_____
_____
_____
_____

Reflections

_____
_____
_____
_____
_____

Thank You For

_____
_____
_____
_____

Personal Challenges

_____
_____
_____
_____

Society And Government

_____
_____
_____
_____

Date

_____

People To Pray For

_____
_____
_____
_____
_____
_____
_____
_____
_____
_____

Reflections

_____
_____
_____
_____
_____

Thank You For

_____

_____

_____

_____

Personal Challenges

_____

_____

_____

_____

Society And Government

_____

_____

_____

_____

Reflections

_____

_____

_____

_____

Date

_____

People To Pray For

_____

_____

_____

_____

_____

_____

_____

_____

_____

_____

Thank You For

_____

_____

_____

_____

Personal Challenges

_____

_____

_____

_____

_____

Society And Government

_____

_____

_____

_____

Date

_____

People To Pray For

_____

_____

_____

_____

_____

_____

_____

_____

_____

_____

Reflections

_____

_____

_____

_____

_____

Thank You For

_____
_____
_____
_____

Personal Challenges

_____
_____
_____
_____

Society And Government

_____
_____
_____
_____

Reflections

_____
_____
_____
_____

Date

_____

People To Pray For

_____
_____
_____
_____
_____
_____
_____
_____
_____
_____
_____

Thank You For

_____
_____
_____
_____

Personal Challenges

_____
_____
_____
_____

Society And Government

_____
_____
_____
_____

Date

_____

People To Pray For

_____
_____
_____
_____
_____
_____
_____
_____
_____
_____
_____

Reflections

_____
_____
_____
_____
_____

Thank You For

_____
_____
_____
_____

Personal Challenges

_____
_____
_____
_____

Society And Government

_____
_____
_____
_____

Reflections

_____
_____
_____
_____

Date

_____

People To Pray For

_____
_____
_____
_____
_____
_____
_____
_____
_____
_____

Thank You For

_____

_____

_____

_____

Personal Challenges

_____

_____

_____

_____

Society And Government

_____

_____

_____

_____

Reflections

_____

_____

_____

_____

Date

_____

People To Pray For

_____

_____

_____

_____

_____

_____

_____

_____

_____

Thank You For

_____
_____
_____
_____

Personal Challenges

_____
_____
_____
_____

Society And Government

_____
_____
_____
_____

Reflections

_____
_____
_____
_____

Date

_____

People To Pray For

_____
_____
_____
_____
_____
_____
_____
_____
_____
_____
_____

Thank You For

Date

People To Pray For

Personal Challenges

Society And Government

Reflections

Thank You For

_____
_____
_____
_____

Personal Challenges

_____
_____
_____
_____

Society And Government

_____
_____
_____
_____

Date

_____

People To Pray For

_____
_____
_____
_____
_____
_____
_____
_____
_____
_____
_____

Reflections

_____
_____
_____
_____

Thank You For

_____
_____
_____
_____

Personal Challenges

_____
_____
_____
_____

Society And Government

_____
_____
_____
_____

Date

_____

People To Pray For

_____
_____
_____
_____
_____
_____
_____
_____
_____

Reflections

_____
_____
_____
_____
_____

Thank You For

_____
_____
_____
_____

Personal Challenges

_____
_____
_____
_____

Society And Government

_____
_____
_____
_____

Reflections

_____
_____
_____
_____

Date

_____

People To Pray For

_____
_____
_____
_____
_____
_____
_____
_____
_____
_____

Thank You For

_____
_____
_____
_____

Personal Challenges

_____
_____
_____
_____
_____

Society And Government

_____
_____
_____
_____

Date

_____

People To Pray For

_____
_____
_____
_____
_____
_____
_____
_____
_____
_____
_____

Reflections

_____
_____
_____
_____
_____

Thank You For

_____
_____
_____
_____

Personal Challenges

_____
_____
_____
_____
_____

Society And Government

_____
_____
_____
_____

Date

_____

People To Pray For

_____
_____
_____
_____
_____
_____
_____
_____
_____
_____

Reflections

_____
_____
_____
_____
_____

Thank You For

_____
_____
_____
_____

Personal Challenges

_____
_____
_____
_____

Society And Government

_____
_____
_____
_____

Date

_____

People To Pray For

_____
_____
_____
_____
_____
_____
_____
_____
_____

Reflections

_____
_____
_____
_____

Thank You For

Personal Challenges

Society And Government

Reflections

Date

People To Pray For

Thank You For

_____
_____
_____
_____

Date

_____

People To Pray For

_____
_____
_____
_____
_____
_____
_____
_____
_____
_____
_____
_____
_____

Personal Challenges

_____
_____
_____
_____

Society And Government

_____
_____
_____
_____

Reflections

_____
_____
_____
_____

Thank You For

_____
_____
_____
_____

Personal Challenges

_____
_____
_____
_____
_____

Society And Government

_____
_____
_____
_____

Reflections

_____
_____
_____
_____
_____

Date

_____

People To Pray For

_____
_____
_____
_____
_____
_____
_____
_____
_____
_____
_____

Thank You For

_____
_____
_____
_____

Personal Challenges

_____
_____
_____
_____

Society And Government

_____
_____
_____
_____

Date

_____

People To Pray For

_____
_____
_____
_____
_____
_____
_____
_____
_____

Reflections

_____
_____
_____
_____
_____

Thank You For

_____
_____
_____
_____

Personal Challenges

_____
_____
_____
_____

Society And Government

_____
_____
_____
_____

Date

_____

People To Pray For

_____
_____
_____
_____
_____
_____
_____
_____
_____

Reflections

_____
_____
_____
_____

Thank You For

_____

_____

_____

_____

Personal Challenges

_____

_____

_____

_____

Society And Government

_____

_____

_____

_____

Date

_____

People To Pray For

_____

_____

_____

_____

_____

_____

_____

_____

_____

_____

_____

_____

Reflections

_____

_____

_____

_____

Thank You For

_____
_____
_____
_____

Personal Challenges

_____
_____
_____
_____

Society And Government

_____
_____
_____
_____

Reflections

_____
_____
_____
_____
_____

Date

_____

People To Pray For

_____
_____
_____
_____
_____
_____
_____
_____
_____
_____
_____

Thank You For

_____
_____
_____
_____

Date

_____

People To Pray For

_____
_____
_____
_____
_____
_____
_____
_____
_____

Personal Challenges

_____
_____
_____
_____

Society And Government

_____
_____
_____
_____

Reflections

_____
_____
_____
_____

Thank You For

_____
_____
_____
_____

Personal Challenges

_____
_____
_____
_____

Society And Government

_____
_____
_____
_____

Date

_____
_____

People To Pray For

_____
_____
_____
_____
_____
_____
_____
_____
_____
_____
_____

Reflections

_____
_____
_____
_____
_____

Thank You For

_____
_____
_____
_____

Personal Challenges

_____
_____
_____
_____

Society And Government

_____
_____
_____
_____

Reflections

Date

_____

People To Pray For

_____
_____
_____
_____
_____
_____
_____
_____
_____
_____
_____

_____
_____
_____
_____
_____

Thank You For

_____

_____

_____

_____

Personal Challenges

_____

_____

_____

_____

Society And Government

_____

_____

_____

_____

Reflections

_____

_____

_____

_____

_____

Date

_____

People To Pray For

_____

_____

_____

_____

_____

_____

_____

_____

_____

_____

Thank You For

_____
_____
_____
_____

Personal Challenges

_____
_____
_____
_____

Society And Government

_____
_____
_____
_____

Date

_____

People To Pray For

_____
_____
_____
_____
_____
_____
_____
_____
_____
_____

Reflections

_____
_____
_____
_____

Thank You For

_____
_____
_____
_____

Personal Challenges

_____
_____
_____
_____

Society And Government

_____
_____
_____
_____

Reflections

_____
_____
_____
_____
_____

Date

_____

People To Pray For

_____
_____
_____
_____
_____
_____
_____
_____
_____

Thank You For

_____

_____

_____

_____

Date

_____

People To Pray For

_____

_____

_____

_____

_____

_____

_____

_____

_____

_____

_____

Personal Challenges

_____

_____

_____

_____

Society And Government

_____

_____

_____

_____

Reflections

_____

_____

_____

_____

Thank You For

_____

_____

_____

_____

Personal Challenges

_____

_____

_____

_____

Society And Government

_____

_____

_____

_____

Reflections

_____

_____

_____

_____

Date

_____

People To Pray For

_____

_____

_____

_____

_____

_____

_____

_____

_____

_____

_____

Made in the USA
Columbia, SC
28 September 2024